j972
~~330.972~~ Lewington, Anna.
LEW
    Mexico.

98

$24.26

Economically Developing Countries

Mexico

Anna Lewington

RSVP

RAINTREE
STECK-VAUGHN
PUBLISHERS
The Steck-Vaughn Company

Austin, Texas

Economically Developing Countries

Bangladesh
Brazil
China
Egypt
Ghana
India

Korea
Malaysia
Mexico
Nigeria
Peru
Vietnam

Cover: A Mexican farmer waters his sisal crop in the shadow of the Sierra Madre Occidental.

Title page: A cliff diver at Acapulco plunges from a height of one hundred feet into shallow water.

Contents page: Visitors swarm over the massive Aztec Pyramid of the Moon at Teotihuacan.

Picture acknowledgments: All photographs including the cover are by Edward Parker. All artwork by Peter Bull.

Published by Raintree Steck-Vaughn Publishers, an imprint of Steck-Vaughn Company

Library of Congress Cataloging-in-Publication Data
Lewington, Anna.
Mexico / Anna Lewington.
    p.   cm.—(Economically developing countries)
    Includes bibliographical references and index.
    Summary: Discusses the geography, peoples, history, and economy of the different regions of Mexico.
    ISBN 0-8172-4528-6
    1. Mexico—Economic conditions—1982—Juvenile literature.
    2. Mexico—Juvenile literature.
    [1. Mexico.]
    I. Title. II. Series.
    HC135.L47   1996
    330.972—dc20   95-36333

Printed in Italy
1 2 3 4 5 6 7 8 9 0 00 99 98 97 96

Contents

Introduction

Mexico lies between the United States and Central America. To the east of Mexico is the Gulf of Mexico, to the west is the Pacific Ocean. To the south, Mexico has frontiers with two Central American countries—Belize and Guatemala. Mexico shares a border with the United States in the north that stretches for about two thousand miles. Sharing a border with a superpower has had an important effect on the way Mexico has developed.

Despite the strong influence of the United States, Mexico has kept a special identity of its own. Three hundred years as a Spanish colony have left Mexico with a strong Spanish culture, but Mexicans are also proud of their great heritage from indigenous cultures such as the Aztecs, Mayans, and Toltecs.

"I was born in Oaxaca [state] but there were so few jobs there I traveled here [Tijuana] with my family to find work. Some of my family work in the new factories and others work over the border in the United States."
—a Zapotec Indian living in Tijuana

An Indian woman from Oaxaca working as a street seller in the northern city of Tijuana

4

Mexico City, where the wealth of Mexico is concentrated, is the main financial, cultural, and business center of the nation.

As in most Latin-American countries, there are great variations in Mexicans' standards of living. Many people are poor and each year thousands try to enter the United States illegally, in search of the chance for a better life. Mexican history has been shaped by frequent revolutions and uprisings, mostly caused by unfair distribution of land. This unrest continues even today.

Mexico is a wealthy country with great natural resources. It has enormous mineral resources, is one of the world's biggest producers of oil, and is the biggest producer of silver. Mexico is a highly industrialized country, with massive industrial areas surrounding most of the major cities. The spectacular and varied natural beauty of Mexico and its rich cultural history attract millions of tourists each year, making a major contribution to the economy.

5

Landscape

Mexico covers an area of more than 760,000 square miles. Forming a land bridge between the United States and tropical Central America, it is a country of extraordinary variety.

The landscape of Mexico can be divided into three main types: coastal plains, peninsulas, and mountain ranges and plateaus.

Map labels:
Tijuana, BAJA CALIFORNIA, GULF OF CALIFORNIA, COASTAL PLAIN, SIERRA MADRE OCCIDENTAL, Yaquis, San Lorenzo, MEXICAN HIGH PLATEAU, Chihuahua, SIERRA MADRE ORIENTAL, Rio Bravo, Monterrey, COASTAL PLAIN, Tropic of Cancer, CARIBBEAN SEA, GULF OF MEXICO, Merida, YUCATAN PENINSULA, N, Guadalajara, León, Lake Chapala, Mexico City, Puebla, TRANSVOLCANIC MOUNTAIN RANGE, Balsas, Acapulco, Grijalva, Usumacinta

Scale: 0 – 500 – 1000 km / 0 – 300 – 600 miles

COASTAL PLAINS

The coastal plain running along the Gulf of Mexico is characterized by wide beaches, sand bars, swamps, and lagoons and almost no good natural harbors. The climate is generally very hot, with high rainfall in the south and little rainfall in the north. Along the western coast, the plain is widest in the north, where its broad basins are separated by ranges of low hills. Farther south, the plain narrows to little more than a strip, with good natural harbors at Acapulco and Manzanillo. The climate in the north is predominantly hot and dry, with high rainfall below the Tropic of Capricorn.

PENINSULAS

The Yucatán Peninsula is a limestone platform with a gently rolling landscape jutting out into the Gulf of Mexico. There are few rivers and lakes because of the porous nature of the limestone, and the climate is extremely hot with moderate levels of rainfall.

Mexico has a varied landscape ranging from tropical coastlines, like this on the Gulf of Mexico, to snowcapped mountains.

6

Baja California is a thin peninsula of land running south from the northwest corner of Mexico for more than 800 miles, ranging from 30 to 150 miles wide. A series of mountain ranges run down the middle, and there are semidesert and desert coastlines. Baja California has little rainfall and the temperatures vary from close to freezing in winter to over 100°F in summer.

MOUNTAIN RANGES AND PLATEAUS

Mexico is a mountainous country and the average altitude is more than 3,300 feet. Two mountain ranges dominate north and central Mexico, running down either side of the country roughly parallel with the coasts—the Sierra Madre Occidental in the west and the Sierra Madre Oriental in the east. These enclose the vast tablelands that make up the Mexican High Plateau. In the north, the conditions are very arid, with large expanses of desert, generally hot temperatures, and low annual rainfall. Winter temperatures are affected by Arctic winds from the north and can fall to freezing. The southern plateau has abundant rains and a more temperate climate.

Another mountainous feature is the Transvolcanic Mountain Range, which runs virtually the width of the country just south of Mexico City. It is a complex of high plateaus, valleys, lakes, and volcanoes, and includes the nation's highest mountain, Citlaltépetl, also called Pico de Orizaba, which is 18,700 feet high.

The volcano Popocatépetl last erupted in the spring of 1995. It had been thought that the volcano was extinct.

People

Most of Mexico's 86.5 million people live in the high plateau area in the center of the country. Just about one-fourth of all Mexicans live in the Mexico City area. Mexico's population continues to grow rapidly, although measures to control it have decreased the growth rate from over 3.5 percent in the 1970s to close to 2 percent in 1991.

FIRST PEOPLE AND FIRST SETTLERS

Some of the world's greatest civilizations developed in Mexico and Central America. Between 1200 B.C. and the sixteenth century, Mexico was home to a succession of Indian civilizations, such as the Olmec, Maya, Zapotec, Mixtec, and Toltec. They reached high levels of artistic and scientific achievement and were to influence not only Mexican culture but the development of human knowledge worldwide.

The last great civilization was that of the Aztecs, who appeared in the early fourteenth century and by the early sixteenth century controlled most of central Mexico. In 1519 Spanish conquistador Hernan Cortéz arrived in Mexico with a small army in search of conquest. With the help of other Indian groups who were already resisting Aztec domination, Cortéz was able to overthrow the Aztec empire, which was led by Montezuma.

Below *Very little is known about the Olmecs, who carved ten-ton stone heads like this one. The heads are made of basalt, a rock that is not found in eastern Mexico.*

During the initial period of colonization, disease, war, and slavery wiped out huge numbers of indigenous people. It is estimated that, at the beginning of the sixteenth century, there were about 25 million Indians in Mexico and Central America; today, about 7.5 million remain. There are 56 distinct indigenous groups in Mexico today, forming about 9 percent of the population. During 300 years of Spanish rule, the European colonists married local people, and mixed-race Spanish-Indians, known as *Mestizos*, now constitute some 60 percent of the population. About 50 indigenous languages are spoken in Mexico, but only 7 are widely used and many are spoken by relatively small numbers of people—for example, fewer than 300 Mexicans now speak Seri. However, 95 percent of the population speaks Spanish, making Mexico the world's largest Spanish-speaking country.

Above *This Totonac man is climbing a pole during a traditional ritual. The Totonacs are just one of 56 different Indian peoples living in Mexico today.*

Right Mestizos *are people of mixed race—part Indian, part European. This* mestizo *woman is selling coconut bread on the beach at Acapulco.*

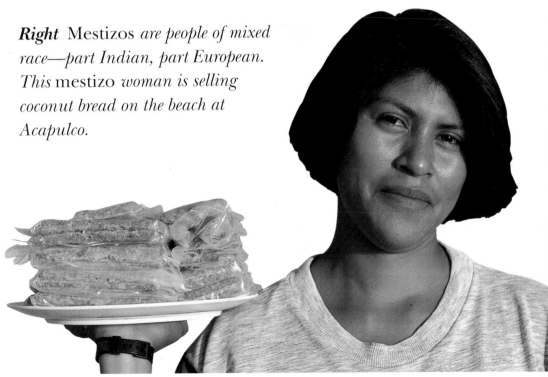

MIGRATIONS

Mexico has a long history of migration and emigration, which continues today. For example, in 1950 about 43 percent of the nation's population was living in urban areas, but by 1990 this figure had risen to 72 percent. In many Mexican states the population is falling as people move to areas with better employment opportunities or because they are forced off their land. The towns with the fastest-growing populations are those along the border with the United States.

People have been migrating from Mexico to the United States since the mid 1800s. In 1901 about 500 people moved to the United States, but by 1991 this figure had risen to 946,167. At the same time, however, an unknown number of Mexicans were entering the United States illegally, and the total number living in the United States today is estimated to be between 1.5 and 3 million.

Less well known is the migration to Mexico by people escaping war, poverty, and human rights abuses in Central American countries. Presently there are about 45,000 officially registered Guatemalan refugees in camps in the southern states of Mexico and probably more than 100,000 undocumented. Another 40,000 to 60,000 Guatemalans cross the border into Mexico every autumn to work on the coffee harvest; most return to Guatemala.

Below A balloon seller in Orizaba

"It doesn't matter how many times you catch me, I'll be back."
—a young Mexican who had just been caught and handcuffed by a Border Patrol agent as he tried to cross the border into the United States illegally

Opposite A view of the sacred Teotihuacan archaeological site, seen from the Pyramid of the Sun. This is where the Aztecs worshiped and carried out human sacrifices.

The Meteoric Rise of the Aztecs

When the Aztecs arrived on the shores of Lake Texcoco, the site of present-day Mexico City, it is said that they were dressed in animal skins and had little technical expertise. Here, they lived off fish, snakes, ducks, and even mosquito larvae. They learned new skills from their neighbors and developed *chinampas*, floating gardens anchored to the lake bottom.

When the local ruler, Azcapotzalco, died in 1428, the Aztecs gained their independence. By 1469, led by Montezuma, the Aztecs had established absolute control of their new land. They became famous as warriors and for human sacrifices. Under Montezuma II, they created a well-organized society where each citizen knew his or her role. The Aztecs provided a system of education never seen in the Americas before. They encouraged art and abstract thought and philosophy. By the time the Spanish arrived in Mexico, the capital city of Tenochtitlán was estimated to have a population of as many as 300,000 inhabitants. It had taken less than one century for the Aztecs to develop from unskilled nomads into one of history's greatest civilizations.

Development

A painting showing the arrival of conquistadors in Mexico in the early sixteenth century. Mexico was a Spanish colony until 1821.

Mexico is a highly industrialized country and has a well-developed economy compared to most developing nations. Unfortunately, this wealth is unevenly distributed and, although some are rich, millions of Mexicans continue to live in poverty. Mexico's history has alternated between periods in which wealth has been concentrated in the hands of a few and periods when genuine attempts have been made to improve the lives of the poor.

THE COLONIAL ERA

The Spanish colonial era lasted for three centuries, during which time the economy was organized solely for the benefit of Spain. Settlers were given grants of land called *encomiendas,* along with Indians to work on them. These soon gave way to *haciendas*— larger areas used for plantations and ranching. The Indians were driven off their land and those who worked for the colonists were severely mistreated.

Spain ruthlessly organized Mexico for maximum profit and minimum competition. For most of the colonial era, Mexico's main agricultural products were corn, cotton cloth, vanilla, indigo (blue dye), cochineal (red dye), and sugar. Mining soon became important. By 1800, for example, Mexico was producing 66 percent of the world's silver.

The influence of the French Revolution led to a series of bloody wars in the early nineteenth century, and on September 27, 1821, Mexico gained independence.

FROM INDEPENDENCE TO REVOLUTION

The first half of the nineteenth century was a time of bloodshed and turmoil that left the country devastated and the economy ruined. Mexico gained independence from Spain in 1821 and, from 1846 to 1848, was involved in a disastrous war with the United States, resulting in the loss of approximately half of its territory. In 1858 war broke out between the Liberals, who were in power, and the Conservatives. Benito Juárez took over the presidency, but the war bankrupted the country once more. In 1861, after borrowing money from Europe, Mexico was unable to pay its debts. Napoleon III used this as an excuse to invade Mexico and appoint Archduke Maximilian of Austria to rule on his behalf. In June of 1867 French troops were forced to leave, and Maximilian was captured and executed. Juárez returned from exile to become President again.

From 1876 until 1911, President Porfirio Diaz ruled the country as a virtual dictator. The economy developed, and a small minority of people became very wealthy. But the majority of the population were close to starvation. These injustices led to revolution.

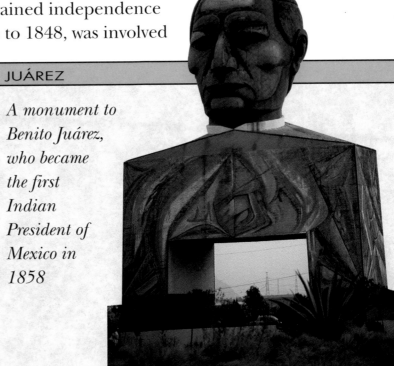

JUÁREZ

A monument to Benito Juárez, who became the first Indian President of Mexico in 1858

One of the greatest heroes of Mexican politics is Benito Pablo Juárez. Born in 1806, he was a Zapotec Indian from Oaxaca and spoke only the Zapotec language as a child. When he became a servant in the home of a wealthy man, he impressed his master so much that he was given an education. He became a lawyer and, in 1847, became Governor of Oaxaca state. Several years later, Juárez was expelled from Mexico because of his opposition to then-president Antonio López de Santa Anna. With a change of government from Conservative to Liberal, Juárez returned to Mexico and became Minister of Justice. It was in this post that he drafted the Ley Juárez, or Juárez Law, of 1857, which has profoundly affected Mexican politics ever since. The law emphasized human rights and land reform and upset the Conservatives by transferring power from the white elite to the *mestizos*. In 1858 Juárez became the first Indian President of Mexico. He died in 1872.

13

REVOLUTION AND ITS AFTERMATH

The Mexican Revolution was not a general uprising against the wealthy but was the result of deeply felt resentment against President Diaz. Although army leaders such as Carranza, Obregón, and Huerta simply wanted power for themselves, popular heroes like Pancho Villa and Emiliano Zapata wanted to change society and redistribute wealth.

In 1911 Diaz was forced out of power, but it was only in 1917, after seven years of war in which over one million Mexicans died, that Mexico obtained a new constitution. The constitution included provisions for human rights and land reform (the redistribution of land) in an attempt to bring peace to the nation. By 1929, several political groups had joined to form the Revolutionary Party, which has ruled Mexico ever since. The land reforms undertaken after the new constitution and during the 1920s are still fiercely defended by poor rural Mexicans today.

A view of the financial sector in Mexico City, the largest financial center of any country in Latin America. Mexico City is second only to Tokyo in population.

MODERNIZATION

World War II forced Mexico to produce what the country needed rather than depending on imports. Many of the raw materials used in arms for the U.S. war effort came also from Mexico, boosting trade.

When President Miguel Alemán Valdés took office in 1946, he concentrated on improving education and attracting foreign investment into Mexican industries such as mining and the automobile industry. This set the scene for rapid development of the economy. Unlike many other countries, Mexico has tried to retain the ideals of the Revolution, and postwar presidents have tried to promote industry while at the same time meeting the people's demands for education and economic opportunity for the poor.

Over the last fifty years, Mexico's single most important export has been oil. In 1982 a glut of oil on the world market caused the collapse of Mexico's economy. Mexico stopped repaying its debts and, in return for further loans, the International Monetary Fund (IMF) forced the Mexican Government to cut its spending by stopping subsidies on essential foods such as milk and corn, causing hardship for millions of Mexicans. A further setback was a major earthquake, which hit Mexico City in 1985, ruining chances of an early return to prosperity.

A refinery rises up behind the oil town of Minatitlán in Tabasco state.

A CHALLENGING FUTURE

Over the last 75 years Mexico has dramatically improved not only its economy but also its education and health systems, which are now among the best of any developing nation. The main improvements, though, have been made in urban areas, and large numbers of rural Mexicans have access only to minimal health care and education.

Over the past decade Mexico has been trying to give the impression that it is a developed nation. Unfortunately, there is a sharp divide between the rich and the poor, which was highlighted by an uprising in Chiapas in 1994.

This division between rich and poor grew during the presidency of Carlos Salinas de Gortiari, which ended in 1994. The number of Mexican billionaires jumped from two to twenty-six, but the World Health Organization estimated in 1992 that more than 40 percent of Mexicans were undernourished.

Mexico has had to increase its foreign debt by $20 billion. This has led to pressure from foreign countries and banks to cut spending on housing, education, and health and to use more land for export crops. For many Mexicans, the standard of living will fall over the next decade.

A shantytown in Tijuana

ECONOMIC AND SOCIAL INDICATORS		
Life Expectancy[1]:	Female—74 years	
	Male—67 years	
Infant Mortality[2]:	0–1 year: 24 per 1,000 (1990)	
Literacy[1]:	88% (1990)	
Gross Domestic Product (size of the economy)[1]:	$358 billion	
Main Sectors of the Economy[2]:		
Commerce, restaurants, hotels		26.0%
Manufacturing		22.7%
Public and private services		17.4%
Financial services, insurance		10.8%
Agriculture, forestry, fishing		8.5%
Other		14.6%
Exports[2]:	$51,833 million	
Imports[2]:	$65,367 million	
Total External Debt[2]:	$135 billion	
Per Capita Income[1]:	$7,490 per year	

Sources: [1]*World Development Report, 1993–94*
[2]*Economist Intelligence Unit Reports (1993)*

NAFTA

On January 1, 1994, Mexico, the United States, and Canada signed the North American Free Trade Agreement (NAFTA). Over the next 15 years, they aim to dismantle all trade barriers between their countries, so that goods can go from one to another without an increase in price.

NAFTA, when completed, will create one of the largest free trade areas in the world.

Tourism in Quintana Roo. In 1993, tourism earned $4 billion.

CORRUPTION AND THE PRESIDENT

Corruption is an ever-present theme in Mexican politics. This story is typical. In June 1995, the former President of Mexico, Carlos Salinas de Gortiari, disappeared from his job at Dow Jones on Wall Street in New York City amid reports that he might be connected to the murder of Francisco Ruiz Massieu, president of the ruling Institutional Revolutionary Party (IRP). Salinas's brother, Raul, has already been charged with masterminding the murder.

Earlier in 1995, the brother of Francisco Ruiz Massieu, Mario, the former Attorney General, was found to have $7 billion in U.S. bank accounts. This led some investigators to speculate that Mario Ruiz Massieu may have been in the pay of drug traffickers.

"It is terrible to think that Salinas [Mexico's president, 1988–1994] was being considered for the post of head of the World Trade Organization when millions of people face starvation in Mexico."
—newspaper seller in Chihuahua

Protesters in Mexico City campaigning against political corruption

Central and Western Regions

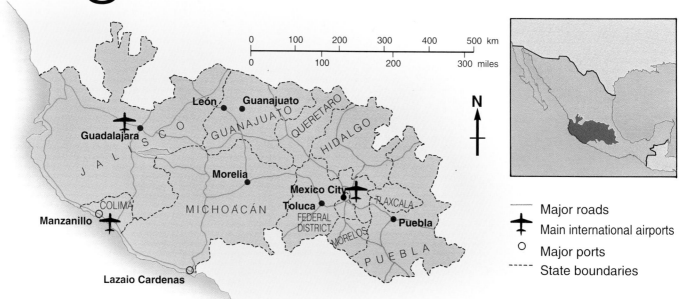

Major roads

Main international airports

Major ports

State boundaries

POPULATION

With its temperate climate and good rainfall, Central Mexico has been the most densely populated area of the Americas for thousands of years. Today, the majority of Mexicans live here, and the Mexico City area alone accounts for a quarter of the entire population. Four of Mexico's six largest cities are found in the

CENTRAL AND WESTERN FACT BOX

Proportion of Mexico Covered: 14.21% (108,156 sq. miles)

Proportion of Mexico's Population: 53% (45,845,000 people)

Population by state (inhabitants per square mile):

Aguascalientes	335	México	1,184
Colima	205	Michoacán	153
Federal District	14,230	Morelos	627
Guanajuato	337	Puebla	316
Hidalgo	233	Querétaro	231
Jalisco	171	Tlaxcala	505

Economy: Wealthiest and most industrialized regions in Mexico

Climate: Temperate

Rainfall: 40–80 inches per year

Source: *Geografia de Mexico* (Trillas, 1994)

Central and Western regions—Mexico City, Guadalajara, Puebla, and León. The population density is high; the Central region has 250 to 1,500 people per square mile, but the West has a lower density of 100 to 250 people per square mile.

A view over Puebla shows the flatness of the tablelands of the Mexican High Plateau.

There are eight indigenous peoples in the Central and Western regions. The largest group is the Nahua—the descendants of the Aztecs—who number over one million. The Aztec language, Nahuatl, is still widely used outside the urban areas.

A Tarascan Indian herbalist sells seeds to ward off evil spirits.

AN ECONOMIC POWERHOUSE

The temperate climate makes this one of the best agricultural areas in Mexico. Although it is declining in importance, agriculture is still a major source of employment. Corn, wheat, and alfalfa are important in the central highlands, giving way to sugarcane, oranges, avocados, strawberries, and other types of fruit in the wetter west.

The main part of the economy, however, is manufacturing. There is a large automobile industry, with factories for Volkswagen in Puebla, Nissan in Cuernavaca, and Ford and General Motors in Mexico City. Chemical and plastics factories are found in the industrial parks that surround most of the major cities.

Every year, more than 100 million monarch butterflies make the hazardous migration from Canada and the United States to spend the winter in two small areas of the Oyamel fir forest in the Sierra Chincua, Michoacán state. Why the butterflies should make this journey of several thousand miles to this tiny area of Mexico remains a mystery. Nobody knows how the butterflies navigate so precisely to the same spot every year.

The areas where the butterflies gather have been made official sanctuaries, and thousands of tourists visit the two areas, which helps the local economy.

SOCIAL CONDITIONS

The living conditions of Mexicans vary greatly in the Central and Western regions. In the big cities there are zones of great wealth, where living standards are like the best in Europe or the United States. However, there are also districts—often close to these wealthy areas—where even the basic amenities of clean water and sewers are not available to the inhabitants.

Over the last few decades, the middle class, made up of professionals such as teachers and engineers, has been growing and makes up a larger part of the population than in other regions. However, the rural population and the indigenous people, as in the other regions, have least access to health and education. All inhabitants of the large cities suffer to a greater or lesser extent from the high levels of pollution and social problems such as violent crime.

"I am a guitarist with a mariachi band. We usually wait around the Plaza Garibaldi for cars or taxis sent to pick us up to go and play at parties…since the problems with the economy [1995] there has been very little work."
—a mariachi musician from Mexico City

Mariachi musicians like this man have provided entertainment in Mexico since the 1920s.

> *"The monarch butterflies are a gift from God...More than one hundred million migrate every year from Canada to this valley [in Sierra Chincua, Michoacán state]...without the thousands of tourists who come to the Monarch Butterfly Sanctuary, we would just be poor farmers or would have to leave the area to find work."*
> **—a guide at the Monarch Butterfly Sanctuary**

Between January and March every year, millions of monarch butterflies can be seen in the Sierra Chincua. They often gather in one small area or around a single tree.

Mexican food for the world

When people think of Mexican food they often think of spicy meat dishes with hot chili peppers, such as Chili con Carne. However, most Europeans and North Americans eat Mexican food every day without realizing it, for many commonly eaten foods originated in Mexico.

When Cortéz conquered Mexico, he was hoping to find great riches in the form of gold and silver to send back to Spain. However, it was the new food plants that now form part of Western diets that proved far more lasting than Mexico's mineral wealth. The first and most important plant to be exported was corn. In the sixteenth century, Europe still suffered from famines but, with the introduction of corn from Mexico and potatoes from Peru, these became far less frequent.

Other crops from Mexico that now contribute to a multibillion-dollar world food industry are cocoa, chili peppers, tomatoes, vanilla, chicle latex (used in chewing gum), and avocados.

Chili peppers are a Mexican flavoring now used all over the world.

21

Smog over Mexico City. According to the World Health Organization, Mexico City has the worst air pollution of any city in the world.

THE WORLD'S MOST POLLUTED CITY

Mexico City is the second largest city in the world. It is the heart of the Mexican economy, with a huge industrial and trading center. For example, Mexico City produces more than 40 percent of the nation's industrial output, and most financial institutions have their headquarters there. Mexico City has been one of the traditional destinations for migrants escaping the hardships of subsistence farming in the countryside. Between 1900 and 1990, the population of the urban area in and around Mexico City rose from 344,000 to 20.2 million.

Mexico City is home to about half the nation's manufacturing industry, but 75 percent of Mexico City's air pollution is caused by its three million vehicles. Every day 12,000 tons of pollutants are added to the smog already hanging over the city. The huge problem of air pollution is made worse by the high mountains that surround the city, preventing polluted air from escaping. Serious health problems are caused by inhaling these high levels of poisonous gases. Statistics from the Children's Hospital of Mexico show that lung and sinus problems and severe colds are now the main problems, followed by gastrointestinal infections. The blood of people living in Mexico City has been shown to have more than twice the level of lead found in the world's other major cities. The introduction of electric streetcars and restriction of car use should reduce pollution in the city.

"[In Mexico City] *rush hour is between 6 A.M. and 9 A.M. in the morning and 6 P.M. and 9 P.M. in the evening…each year the traffic gets worse, and when there has been no rain for a while the pollution is so bad that it is difficult to breathe at times.*"—**Taxi driver in Mexico City**

About 30 percent of Mexico City's population live without access to sewer facilities and the effluent flows untreated into the rivers and waterways. The Panuco River receives about 690,000 tons of untreated sewage a year. The inhabitants of Mexico City also produce 7,000 tons of garbage daily, of which only 75 percent is collected.

A major earthquake hit Mexico City in 1985. About 8,000 people were killed, and millions of dollars of damage were caused.

Hundreds of families live in the garbage dumps of Mexico City. They sort through the debris in search of items that they can sell in order to make a living.

"I live with my family on the garbage dump. It is very difficult to make enough money to feed us…for each cartload of trash I collect, I am paid one peso."—**a man living in one of Mexico City's garbage dumps**

The Gulf and Southeast Regions

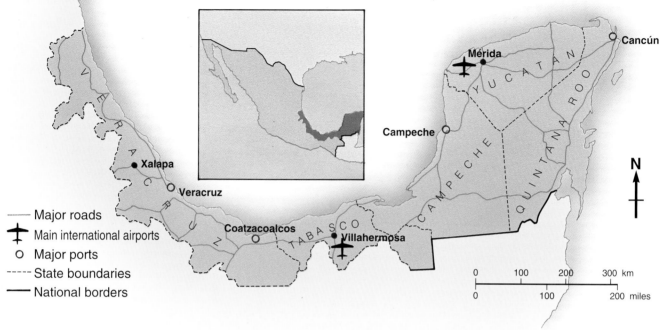

Major roads
Main international airports
Major ports
State boundaries
National borders

MAYAS AND MODERN MEXICANS

The population of the states of Veracruz and Tabasco is 7.7 million; the total population of the three states that comprise the Yucatán Peninsula is only 2.4 million. The Gulf Coast states are home to about half a million indigenous people from groups such as the Totonacs, Popoluca, Huasteca, and some of the Nahua, but the majority of the population are *mestizo*.

In Veracruz and Tabasco the sophisticated culture of the Olmecs flourished between 1000 and 500 B.C. before disappearing mysteriously. In contrast, the descendants of the great Mayan civilization are still numerous in the Yucatán Peninsula. The Mayas are the second-largest indigenous group in Mexico, numbering close to a million.

> ### THE GULF AND SOUTHEAST FACT BOX
>
> Proportion of Mexico Covered:
> 12.12% (92,279 square miles)
> Proportion of Mexico's Population:
> 11% (9,515,000 people)
> Population by state (inhabitants per square mile):
>
> | | |
> |---|---|
> | Campeche | 26 |
> | Quintana Roo | 26 |
> | Tabasco | 158 |
> | Veracruz | 223 |
> | Yucatán | 91 |
>
> Economy: Based on oil, tropical agriculture, and tourism
> Climate: Humid tropical
> Rainfall: Ranges from 20–80 inches per year

The Mayas built spectacular pyramids from A.D. 300–900, including this one, the beautiful Chichén Itzá on the Yucatán Peninsula.

OIL AND TOURISM

Veracruz has better soil and more reliable rainfall than the Yucatán Peninsula. Historically this has allowed it to have a much larger agricultural base. Today, Veracruz is the Mexican state that produces the most beef, mangoes, pineapples, bananas, and papayas, as well as being a major producer of tobacco and coffee. Veracruz also has massive reserves of oil and sulfur. As long ago as 1921, Mexico was the second largest producer of oil in the world, the majority coming from the Gulf Coast.

The story of the Yucatán is very different. The first Spanish settlers set up *encomiendas,* using the local Mayan population as virtual slaves on sugarcane plantations and for logging timber such as mahogany. The Yucatán Peninsula was a major producer of sugarcane until the Five Years War (1846–50), when the the Mayan population attempted to drive out the white settlers, largely destroying the sugar and tobacco plantations.

25

Twenty years ago, Cancún was just a small fishing village. Now, scores of hotels stretch for 12 miles along the coast. They accommodate tens of thousands of visitors each year. The choice to develop this resort was made by a computer in the Bank of Mexico. The computer was fed data relating to all possible tourist locations in Mexico and programmed to select the best location.

When work was started on developing Cancún, there was no road system or international airport, but now the municipal infrastructure is equal to the best in Mexico.

As with many developments in Mexico, the local population and the environment have been the losers while tourists and financial institutions have benefited most.

*"When the hotel zone was being built there was plenty of work for me and my friends, but once the construction was finished there has been very little work…the waiters and hotel staff come from other parts of the country."—**a Cancún construction worker***

A first-class hotel near a beach in Cancún

The economy of the Yucatán is now booming once again, following the discovery of massive oil fields in the Gulf of Mexico and as a result of increased tourism. Cattle ranching is also an important economic activity.

Tabasco is one of the largest producers of coffee, tobacco, bananas, and watermelons and has significant onshore oil reserves and oil refining and petrochemical industries.

Fishing and forestry are also important to the economy of all the Gulf Coast states.

The Gulf Coast states experience regular hurricanes, which, on occasion, devastate large areas of the coast and cause millions of dollars in damage.

Mexico has been a major oil producer for most of the twentieth century—by the 1920s it was the second largest producer in the world. Since the discovery of the rich Reforma oil field in 1972, Mexico has become the world's fifth-largest producer and has the seventh-largest reserves.

In 1988 the three Gulf Coast states accounted for 98 percent of the nation's crude oil and natural gas production. The total number of people employed in the oil industry in these states was approximately 50,000.

When Mexican motorists buy gasoline, there is only one brand and one price. The oil industry has been run by the state-owned Petroleos Mexicanos (Pemex) since March 1938, when President Lázaro Cardenas became a national hero by expelling U.S. and British oil companies from Mexico. Some critics consider Pemex to be too large and powerful and condemn its unregulated pollution and serious accidents caused by unsafe practices.

Above A "nodding donkey" pumps oil out of the ground in Veracruz.

Below A boy at school near Mérida, Yucatán

"There is compulsory education for all children between six and fourteen years of age…as you can see we do not have much money or equipment and … we also do not have enough rooms, so some of the classes are held outside."—**Segundo Marquez, a schoolteacher from Mérida**

POOR SOCIAL CONDITIONS

The social conditions throughout this region are poor. It is home to many agricultural workers, who have little job security and work for close to the minimum wage of 16.5 pesos (about $3) a day. The boom in oil production has increased the cost of living, and tropical diseases such as malaria are prevalent.

Literacy levels in the area are low—for example, in Veracruz, 18.2 percent of the population over 15 years of age is unable to read and write, compared to 4 percent in Mexico City.

Sisal

Above *Sisal fibers drying on racks near Mérida, Yucatán*

Below *This sisal worker, like many others, works hard for very little pay.*

Following the Five Years War, the Yucatán Peninsula's economy was in decline as a result of the destruction of the valuable sugarcane plantations. Ironically, it was the traditional Mayan crop of *henequen* (sisal) that revitalized the flagging economy. The sisal plant is drought-resistant and ideally suited to the Yucatán. The pulp is scraped from the leaves and the fiber woven into rope. Between 1875 and 1916 the demand for sisal rose dramatically, but once again the Mayan Indians were exploited to provide the labor. In the 1920s, plastics began to replace sisal rope, with detrimental effects on the economy of the Yucatán Peninsula. The Yucatán is still the leading producer of sisal but it no longer has a monopoly, having to compete with Brazil and Tanzania.

"I work here in the sisal-processing plant and my job is to hang the wet sisal fibers out to dry in the sun. I work from three in the morning until eleven A.M., with a break for breakfast at eight. It's heavy work and I earn 18 pesos a day."—**Luiz Rey, a Mayan Indian, working near Mérida, in the Yucatán Peninsula, March 1995**

28

The Northwest

INCREASING POPULATION

This region has a very low population density, with the states of Sonora and Baja California Sur having only 10 to 30 people per square mile. At the same time, the migration of people from the poor southern states is particularly high, especially to the cities close to the American border.

Formerly, there were numerous Indian peoples in this region, including the Apaches, but through disease and war the numbers have been greatly reduced. There are now only a few hundred Indians in the Baja California peninsula. In Sonora the Seri Indians, who once numbered many thousands, have been reduced to three hundred.

Mexicali
Tijuana
BAJA CALIFORNIA NORTE
BAJA CALIFORNIA SUR
SONORA
Guaymas
La Paz
Culiacán
SINALOA
Mazatlán
NAYARIT

0 100 200 300 km
0 100 200 miles

—— Major roads
✈ Main international airports
○ Major ports
---- State boundaries
—— National borders

N

NORTHWEST FACT BOX

Proportion of Mexico Covered:	21.26%
(161,916 square miles)	
Proportion of Mexico's Population:	8.6%
(7,439,000 people)	

Population by state (inhabitants per square mile):

Baja California Norte	62
Baja California Sur	10
Nayarit	78
Sinaloa	98
Sonora	26

Economy:	Industrial development, tourism, mechanized agriculture, and fishing
Climate:	Hot and dry
Average Rainfall:	Less than 20 inches per year

The arid landscape of Baja California

FARM WORKERS AT RISK

As elsewhere in Mexico, access to education and health care has been improved over the last two decades. The region has the second-highest level of literacy in the country, and hospital and other social services are among the best in Mexico.

However, the large influx of migrant workers into cities like Tijuana has put new strains on social services. Also, a combination of rapid industrialization and population growth has increased pollution. The result is that increasing numbers of people do not have access to clean water. There are also health problems for the workers on the big agricultural estates of the region, who suffer from exposure to high levels of pesticides.

Above A Seri wearing a traditional headdress. Only about three hundred Seris remain in Sonora state.

THE INFLUENCE OF THE UNITED STATES

The economy of the area is one of the fastest growing in Mexico. There are a range of economic activities that are influenced by the region's proximity to the United States.

The region has a huge agricultural economy producing tomatoes and other soft fruit and vegetables for the United States. There are also large areas of cotton, corn, wheat, and sugar. The fishing industry is a traditionally strong part of the economy and, although there is little oil in the region, Sonora state has Mexico's largest copper mine. Tourism plays an increasingly important role in the economy of Baja California Norte.

Left Workers from a tomato farm in Baja California collect their wages at the end of the day. These workers regularly work in temperatures exceeding 90°F.

CHICKEN FEED

Much of the agriculture in the Northeast has been developed specifically to meet the demands of the United States. Enormous fields of marigolds supply the U.S. poultry industry. The yellow flower heads are fed to chickens during the winter months. American consumers prefer eggs with bright yellow yolks all year round, and the marigolds are added to chicken feed to color the egg yolks.

Right   These marigolds, grown near Los Mochis in Sinaloa state, are destined to become chicken food on U.S. farms.

> *"I work planting and picking tomatoes, chilis, and grapes. It is very hot work in the fields and in the summer it is often 105°F by 11 A.M. ... I earn about $5 a day."*
> **—Filiberto de la Luis, agricultural worker, Baja California Norte**

Left   Tomatoes and limes from Mexico. Tomato exports earn over $200 million annually.

31

TOURISTS

Tourism is an important part of the economy of the northwest. Tijuana alone is visited by as many as forty million tourists every year. Most of these just come for a day to buy items, such as jeans and shoes, that are often cheaper than in the United States. Car repair is another thing on which day-trippers spend their money.

The whole of Baja California Norte is geared toward catering to tourists, mainly from the United States. At Laguna Ojo de Liebre, sometimes called Scammons Lagoon, near Guerro Negro, hundreds of gray whales come to breed every spring, and many visitors have a chance to see whales for the first time. The region is also a popular destination for thousands of people with mobile homes, who head south from all over the United States.

Until recently, the Baja peninsula was relatively isolated. The completion of a good road for virtually the whole of its eight-hundred-mile length has stimulated tourism. This, in turn, has created a booming economy, causing an influx of migrants from the poorer states who come in search of work.

A blanket seller walks between tourists' cars as they cross the border from Tijuana back into the United States.

Tourists head out to sea, hoping to see gray whales in Laguna Ojo de Liebre, Baja California Norte.

"I am 19 years old and my brother and I moved from Oaxaca to Tijuana two years ago. There was no work in Oaxaca but now I have a job in a Japanese television company as an electrician. I earn about $40 a week, but I am hoping that one day I can work in the U.S. where people get much more money for the same job."
—Hermillo Reyes

Maquilladora

The *maquilladora,* or "in-bond" industries, are the fastest-growing sector of the Mexican economy. These industries make well-known brand-name items for foreign companies, for sale mainly in the United States. The factories are set up using a combination of Mexican and foreign money. The advantage to the foreign countries involved is that products can be made much more cheaply in Mexico, while Mexico benefits from the employment created. Some critics argue that the cost savings are made at the expense of the Mexican workers and the environment. This is because there are fewer regulations on pollution and working conditions in Mexico.

At the end of 1992 there were over 2,070 *maquilladora* businesses in operation, employing 504,000 people, both in the original zone along the Mexico-U.S. border and now farther south in Mexico. The principal activities are the assembly of motor vehicles, electrical goods, electronics, furniture, chemicals, and textiles.

Workers at a maquilladora Japanese TV factory having lunch at a taco stand.

Shrinking shrimp

The Sea of Cortéz, also known as the Gulf of California, is rich in fish stocks. It is popular for sport fishing, especially for marlin, but it is also renowned for its giant shrimp. Every year between October and March thousands of tons of Pacific shrimp are caught, packed in ice, and exported to the United States. It is one of the most valuable catches in terms of dollars per pound and makes a major contribution to the region's economy. However, the numbers of shrimp are decreasing because of overfishing. It is feared that many of the estimated 350 fish species that inhabit the Sea of Cortéz will face extinction if overfishing continues.

"Shrimp are the most valuable catch from the Gulf of California, and my family has made a good living from shrimping for many years…recently it has become more difficult to catch shrimp and we have to spend more time at sea than before."
—the captain of a shrimp boat on the Sea of Cortéz

Above *Stocks of Pacific shrimp are declining because of overfishing.*

Left *A shrimp boat returns to Guaymas harbor with its catch.*

Pacific South

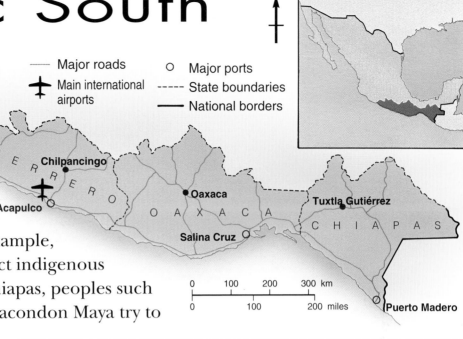

Map Legend:
— Major roads
✈ Main international airports
○ Major ports
----- State boundaries
— National borders

INDIGENOUS PEOPLES

The population of the three states that make up this region has a high proportion of indigenous people. In the state of Oaxaca, for example, there are seventeen distinct indigenous peoples. In the state of Chiapas, peoples such as Tzotzils, Tzeltals, and Lacondon Maya try to maintain a traditional lifestyle in the rain forest.

The population density is low and there are few large cities. Acapulco is the only city nearing one million inhabitants. Migration of people has become a significant feature of the area, both from the countryside to the cities and out of the region to areas such as central Mexico, cities close to the U.S. border (such as Tijuana), and areas of tourist growth such as Quintana Roo, where job prospects are better. The migration of young people out of the area causes social problems, since only the elderly are left behind.

PACIFIC SOUTH FACT BOX

Proportion of Mexico Covered: 11.81%
(89,979 square miles)

Proportion of Mexico's Population: 9.4%
(8,131,000 people)

Population by state (inhabitants per square mile):

Chiapas	112
Guerrero	106
Oaxaca	83

Economy: Weakest region, with economy based on plantation agriculture, mining, forestry, and tourism

Climate: Arid highlands, tropical lowlands

Average Rainfall: 20 inches in north and 80 inches in south

A Zapotec Indian and her daughter set out fruit and vegetables to sell at a market in Oaxaca state.

AGRICULTURE AND TOURISM

The economy of the region is predominantly agricultural, producing coffee, mangoes, bananas, avocados, tobacco, sugar, and honey. Cattle ranching is also important.

There are mineral deposits of fluorite in Chiapas, and metals such as silver, gold, and copper are found in the region, but in smaller quantities than in the north. Chiapas is the nation's main region for hydroelectric power.

Paper mills have been set up throughout the region because of the extensive forests. But there are few large manufacturing or service industries other than tourism, which tends to be concentrated in Acapulco and Oaxaca.

A view of the arid landscape close to Oaxaca City

"We grow the finest Mexican coffee here in Oaxaca [state] *because our fields are the highest and the rains are good."*
—Jose Ramon, a small-scale coffee farmer

Acapulco, the largest city in Guerreo state, and the destination for thousands of tourists each year.

A struggle for rights

On January 1, 1994, hundreds of Indians of Mayan descent—Tzotzils, Tzeltals, Chols, and Tojolabals—staged an armed revolt against the Mexican Government. Peasant farmers joined with the Indians to form the Zapatista National Liberation Army (ZNLA), demanding an end to the "plundering of our natural wealth." The Indian uprising took place in Chiapas, a state with one of the largest gaps between rich and poor in Mexico. For centuries, the Indian people of Chiapas have witnessed the exploitation of their resources and the destruction of their lands, suffering years of oppression and poverty. In the words of the leader of the ZNLA, Subcommandante Marcos, "Chiapas has been bleeding to death in a thousand different ways, paying its tribute to the empires: oil, electricity, money, coffee, bananas…"

For example, Chiapas is the country's main producer of coffee, Mexico's highest-value agricultural export.

Despite their contribution to the economy, the Indians and peasant farmers are exploited and their land rights ignored. Indian land is often taken over forcibly by wealthy landowners who are usually concerned with making a quick profit. Irreparable damage is caused to land that has been carefully managed for centuries.

The Lacondon forest in Chiapas is part of the Gran Peten, now the second-largest rain forest on the continent after the Amazon. It was in this region that the Mayan civilization flourished. Through wise use of the forest, the Mayans could support population densities of up to 1,300 per square mile, far higher than is possible today. The descendants of the great Mayan civilization are now fighting to be acknowledged and respected in their own land.

Campaigners in front of the Presidential Palace in Mexico City seek a peaceful solution to the Chiapas uprising.

THE POOREST REGION IN MEXICO

The Pacific South region is the poorest in Mexico, with only basic health care facilities for many remote communities. Education facilities are inadequate and the three states have the highest rates of illiteracy in Mexico. Chiapas is the worst, with 30 percent of the population over 15 unable to read or write, compared with 4 percent in Mexico City.

The clearing of tropical forests for cattle ranching often has long-term environmental consequences.

The economy is based largely on agricultural plantations, which offer low wages, poor working conditions, and only seasonal work. Chiapas displays some of the worst aspects of a developing country, with a massive gap between the wealthy and the poor, the violent eviction of peasant farmers from their land for plantations, destructive forestry and cattle ranching, and inadequate health and education for the poorest in society. Under the *cacique* system, still operated in Chiapas, bosses are like old colonial masters and the workers are treated as virtual slaves. It is hard for the workers to leave their employment or to demand a fair wage.

*"Oaxaca is much hotter and drier than it used to be ten years ago…that was before the paper mills were built and the forests around the city were cut down."—**Jesus Portilla, taxi driver, Oaxaca***

38

Time calculations of the Mayas

The Mayan culture was at it height between A.D. 300 and 900. During this time, their empire included most of southern Mexico, the Yucatán Peninsula, and large areas of Central America. It was a highly sophisticated agricultural society, capable of astonishing architectural feats such as the pyramid complex of Palenque.

The Mayas developed a method of recording the passage of time. They calculated the year at 365.2420 days and the Moon's orbit as 29.5209 days. Only in the twentieth century did mathematicians calculate more accurate figures. The Mayas measured time from a date "zero" on August 10, 3113 B.C. and predicted that the world would end on December 24, A.D. 2011.

The Mayans were among the first people to invent and use the mathematical concept of zero. They wrote with an advanced hieroglyphic script and created the most advanced and accurate calendar ever used. Unfortunately, the Mayas' books were burned by the priest Diego de Landa in 1562 and he wrote later, "We found many books and they contained nothing but superstitions and lies of the Devil…We burned them all, which grieved the Mayas enormously."

Palenque, one of the finest examples of Mayan architecture in Mexico

The North and Northeast

DECLINING POPULATION

These regions were among the last in Mexico to be colonized, because of the resistance of the Indian populations. However, the lure of the silver mines proved irresistible to the Spaniards, who settled in fortified towns. Marauding bands of Apaches terrorized the settlers for the first 150 years, and uprisings, such as that of the Tarahumara Indians in 1616, also made colonization difficult.

Today, the area is sparsely populated and has vast expanses of semidesert and mountain. The large towns close to the border with the United States are growing rapidly, while the interior states of Zacatecas and San Luis Potosí have declining populations.

The Barranca del Cobre (Copper Canyon) is nearly 330 feet deeper than the Grand Canyon.

0	100 200 300 km	
0	100	200 miles

— Major roads
✈ Main international airports
○ Major ports
- - - State boundaries
—— National borders

N

CHIHUAHUA
Chihuahua
COAHUILA
DURANGO
Saltillo   Monterrey
Durango   NUEVO LEÓN
ZACATECAS
Zacatecas SAN LUIS POTOSÍ
San Luis Potosí   Tampico
AGUASCALIENTES

THE NORTH AND NORTHEAST FACT BOX

Proportion of Mexico Covered: 40.6%
   (309,104 square miles)

Proportion of Mexico's Population: 18%
   (15,570,000 people)

Population by state (inhabitants per square mile):

Chihuahua	26
Coahuila	34
Durango	29
Nuevo León	124
San Luis Potosí	83
Tamaulipas	73
Zacatecas	44

Economy: Rapidly developing industrial zones along the border, mining, and extensive agriculture

Climate: Desert and semidesert, cold winters

Average rainfall: Less than 20 inches per year

NEW INDUSTRY ALONG THE BORDER

Chihuahua state is the richest mining area in Mexico. Its precious metals were the original reason for settlement of the area, but this sector of the economy is declining. Manufacturing and *maquilladora* industries are now the most important part of the Mexican economy, with Monterrey accounting for close to a quarter of Mexico's manufacturing output.

The terrain is not favorable for agriculture but irrigated apple orchards, orange and mandarin groves, vineyards, and extensive cattle rearing provide rural employment.

This Tarahumara Indian is selling handmade items to tourists to supplement her income.

TARAHUMARA—RUNNING OUT OF TIME

The 50,000 Tarahumara (or Raramuri) people live in southwest Chihuahua in the rugged Sierra Occidental mountain range. The Tarahumara took refuge in this remote area centuries ago to escape the Spanish invaders and missionaries. They are famous throughout Mexico for being great athletes and are able to catch deer and other animals on foot, chasing them until the animals collapse from exhaustion.

Ever since the seventeenth century the Tarahumara have had to defend their territory—first from silver miners and then from missionaries and colonists. Today, settlers are still trying to take over their land, mostly for cattle ranching, and a vast forestry project threatens to destroy their forest. Most recently, drug traffickers have moved in, forcing some of the Tarahumara to cultivate and transport drugs. Many have been killed for refusing to assist.

A Tarahumara Indian village

41

GOOD SOCIAL CONDITIONS

The northern states close to the border with the United States have high levels of literacy and good access to health care, while the isolated rural communities and indigenous populations suffer from malnutrition. Monterrey has probably the highest standard of living in the country and employees of large manufacturing companies often enjoy subsidized housing and free health care. Many families have relatives living and working in the United States who send back money to help their families in Mexico. However, this region, like the rest of Mexico, is home for many people who live in poverty.

In many rural villages of the north only the very young and the old remain, because those of working age travel to the cities or the United States to find employment.

BORDER PROBLEMS

U.S. border control police currently catch about one million illegal immigrants each year—15 times more than 30 years ago. The largest cause of migration in Mexico has been the removal of agricultural support to poor farmers. As a consequence, many farmers not only find it hard to earn livings but also to produce crops as cheaply as those grown on large, mechanized farms. This situation could be made worse by the North American Free Trade Agreement (NAFTA), in which Mexico agrees not to protect its farmers from foreign competition. This could lead to the displacement of millions of small-scale farmers and to increased rural unemployment. Migrants could be forced to move into the main urban areas. Traditionally, migrants headed for Mexico City but, because of the severe overcrowding there, the next destination will be the cities of the north, where *maquilladora* industries provide increased employment opportunities.

*"Twelve years ago I was crossing the road when I was hit by a car. I can remember flying through the air and landing on a parked car…I was very badly injured and now I am not able to walk properly. I cannot do a normal job which is why I shine shoes…I earn so little money that I cannot think of marrying and having a family."—**A shoe shine man from Monterrey***

Elderly Mexicans who do not receive government or company pensions are either looked after by their families or have to beg for money.

"We will catch a few [illegal immigrants], *round them up, send them back, but not too many because then who will do the work?"*
—*Representative Esteban E. Torres, a U.S. Congressman (D-California)*

In Mexico, the industrialization of the U.S.–Mexico border has attracted people in search of work. This, in turn, has encouraged migration into the United States. For example, the number of export-assembly plants along the California border with Mexico has quadrupled in the last ten years, and the numbers of people illegally entering the United States have also risen.

At the same time, the economies of the southern United States rely on the cheap labor provided by Mexicans and other migrant workers. Despite the highly mechanized farming methods of the United States, perishable fruit and vegetables are still very labor-intensive crops. Of the two million hired agricultural workers in the United States, Mexicans account for nearly 70 percent. Many of these workers live in appalling conditions and are exposed to high levels of hazardous pesticides. The life expectancy for a migrant farm worker is estimated to be 49 years, 20 years less than the U.S. national average.

The issue of migration is a complex one. Parts of the U.S. economy need migrant workers to remain competitive. In turn, money sent back to Mexico by Mexicans working in the United States is estimated at about $3 billion a year and represents one of Mexico's largest sources of foreign income.

The Future

Mexico has a unique position in the world, sandwiched between an economic superpower and the developing countries of Central America. Other developing nations watch Mexico with interest because there the developed and developing world meet, and the future is being shaped between them.

Mexico City, which is the heart of Mexico's economy, is also at the center of the nation's problems with poverty and pollution.

Over the last fifty years, Mexico has become highly industrialized. But development means more than just improving the economy. It also means raising the living standards of the nation as a whole. While it can be seen that health and education have improved over the last three decades—for example, infant mortality rates have fallen from 69 per 1,000 in 1970 to 27 per 1,000 in 1994—other factors affect the lives of poor and rich alike. Since the 1980s there has been a growing awareness of the environmental cost of uncontrolled economic development and population growth. Poisonous smog hangs over all the major cities and some experts believe that Mexico City could be virtually uninhabitable in just 20 years. In the rush to industrialize, Mexico has polluted the air and water, depleted its fish stocks, and cut down huge areas of forest.

It is important to ask who benefits when there is a period of economic growth. During the 1980s and early 1990s there was growth in the economy, but the majority of Mexicans saw no improvement in their standards of living because each year the price of basic foodstuffs rose faster than the minimum wage. The other question now is whether Mexico will be allowed to spread the wealth more evenly in the future even if it wants to. In 1982, and again in 1995, the Mexican economy collapsed, and Mexico had to borrow billions of dollars from countries like the United States and organizations such as the International Monetary Fund. These loans have certain conditions attached to them that often cause increased hardship to the poorest in society. For example, the 1995 loans specified a reduction in public spending, including spending on housing, health, and education. These measures affect the poor, while the wealthy people who run the country remain largely unaffected.

In the last decade, the rich have become richer and the poor poorer in Mexico. If this trend continues, the country faces the possibility of returning to the conditions of the *Porfiriato* (1876–1911), a dark period of Mexican history under President Porfirio Diaz. Although there was strong economic growth under Diaz , it was also a time of great misery for the majority of Mexicans, brought to an end by the bloody Revolution of 1910–1911.

Mexico still has a great deal in its favor. It is rich in natural resources and has a young, dynamic population. Its proximity to the United States is a great economic advantage. In the past, Mexico has surprised its critics, and it could do so again in the future.

A Mexican family enjoys a day out at the spectacular Teotihuacan archaeological site.

Glossary

Amenities Services or facilities that are useful to the general public.

Arid Very dry. For example, terrain that has little or no vegetation.

Cacique An old term for a boss or head man who has almost absolute authority.

Chinampas A floating garden developed by the Aztecs to grow crops in swampy areas. It has a floating base of grass and soil and is anchored to the lake bottom.

Colonial Regarding one country's attempt to govern, and sometimes to occupy, another.

Conquistador Any of the early Spanish adventurers or explorers who conquered lands in the New World.

Constitution A written record of the principles and rules by which a country or state is governed.

Dictator A ruler with unlimited authority.

Effluent Sewage or industrial waste flowing into a river or sea.

Encomiendas Small pieces of farmland allocated by the King of Spain during colonial times.

Famines Periods when food is very scarce and people die from hunger.

Haciendas Large farms or plantations.

Hieroglyphic Pictures or symbols that stand for words.

Human rights Basic rights to which all people are entitled by international law.

Indigenous People People who were the original inhabitants of a particular region.

Infrastructure The basic economic foundations of a country, such as roads, bridges, sewers, etc.

Investment Money that is put into a business activity in order to make a profit.

Irrigate To water land by the use of channels, sprinklers, pipes, etc.

Inflation A general increase in prices.

Maquilladora A sector of Mexican manufacturing industry that is specifically for the production of foreign brand-name products for sale abroad.

Marauding Roaming around, attacking or plundering.

Mestizo A Spanish word describing people of mixed Indian and European race.

Monopoly The exclusive possession or control of the market in a particular commodity.

Nomads People who do not have any one home location but move regularly.

Porous Letting through air and/or water.

Sisal A drought-resistant plant native to Mexico. The fibers are extracted from the leaves to make rope.

Smog A combination of the words "smoke" and "fog," describing a mixture of pollutants in the air.

Subsidize To contribute to a state or government in order to make a product or service cheaper to use or buy.

Subsistence Regarding farming, this means growing just enough food to survive, without extra for sale or profit.

Temperate Neither extremely hot nor extremely cold.

Tropical climate A climate of constant high temperatures and rainfall, found between the Tropic of Cancer and the Tropic of Capricorn.

Further Information

Addresses

The Mexican Tourist Office, 10100 Santa Monica Boulevard, Los Angeles, CA 90067 has pamphlets and general information on most areas of Mexico.

Mexican Embassy, 1911 Pennsylvania Avenue NW, Washington, DC 20006

Further reading

Chrisp, Peter. *Spanish Conquests in the New World.* Exploration and Encounters. New York: Thomson Learning, 1993.

Hicks, Peter. *The Aztecs.* Look into the Past. New York: Thomson Learning, 1993.

Hooper-Trout, Lawana. *The Maya.* Indians of North America. New York: Chelsea House, 1991.

Howard, John. *Mexico.* Silver Burdett Countries. New York: Silver Burdett, 1992.

Illsley, Linda. *A Taste of Mexico.* Food around the World. New York: Thomson Learning, 1995.

Kalman, Bobbie. *Mexico: The Land.* Lands, Peoples, & Cultures. New York: Crabtree Publishing, 1993.

Martinez, Elizabeth Coonrod. *The Mexican-American Experience.* Coming to America. Brookfield, CT: Millbrook Press, 1995.

Mexico in Pictures. Revised edition. Visual Geography. Minneapolis: Lerner, 1994.

Ragan, John D. *Emiliano Zapata.* World Leaders: Past & Present. New York: Chelsea House, 1989.

Silverthorne, Elizabeth. *Fiesta! Mexico's Great Celebrations.* Brookfield, CT: Millbrook Press, 1992.

Stein, R. Conrad. *The Mexican Revolution 1910–1920.* New York: New Discovery, 1994.

Index

Numbers in **bold** refer to illustrations.